Follow the Leader!

Emma Chichester Clark

Margaret K. McElderry Books

New York   London   Toronto   Sydney   Singapore

for Finn

Margaret K. McElderry Books
An imprint of Simon & Schuster Children's Publishing Division
1230 Avenue of the Americas
New York, New York 10020
Copyright © 1999 by Emma Chichester Clark
First published in Great Britain by Andersen Press
First U.S. edition, 2003
Printed in Italy
2 4 6 8 10 9 7 5 3 1
Library of Congress Cataloging-in-Publication Data
Chichester Clark, Emma.
Follow the leader! / Emma Chichester Clark.
p. cm.
Summary: A boy and his animal friends play a game of follow the leader until a tiger
shows up and wants to play too.
ISBN 0-689-84296-1
[1. Animals—Fiction. 2. Tigers—Fiction. 3. Games—Fiction.] I. Title.

PZ7.C4328 Fo 2003
[E]—dc21
2002005902

Along the path,
hopping and skipping,
follow the leader!

Through the trees,
whirling and twirling,
follow the leader!

Over the stile,
leaping and bounding,
follow the leader!

Up the hill,
puffing and panting,
follow the leader!

But wait. . . .
Can you hear it?
Shhh! What's that noise?

RRROOO

Round the corner,
jumping and jiving,
follow the leader!

Down the steps,
bumping and thumping,
follow the leader!

Across the stream,
splishing and splashing,
follow the leader!

Into the woods,
shouting and roaring,
follow the leader!

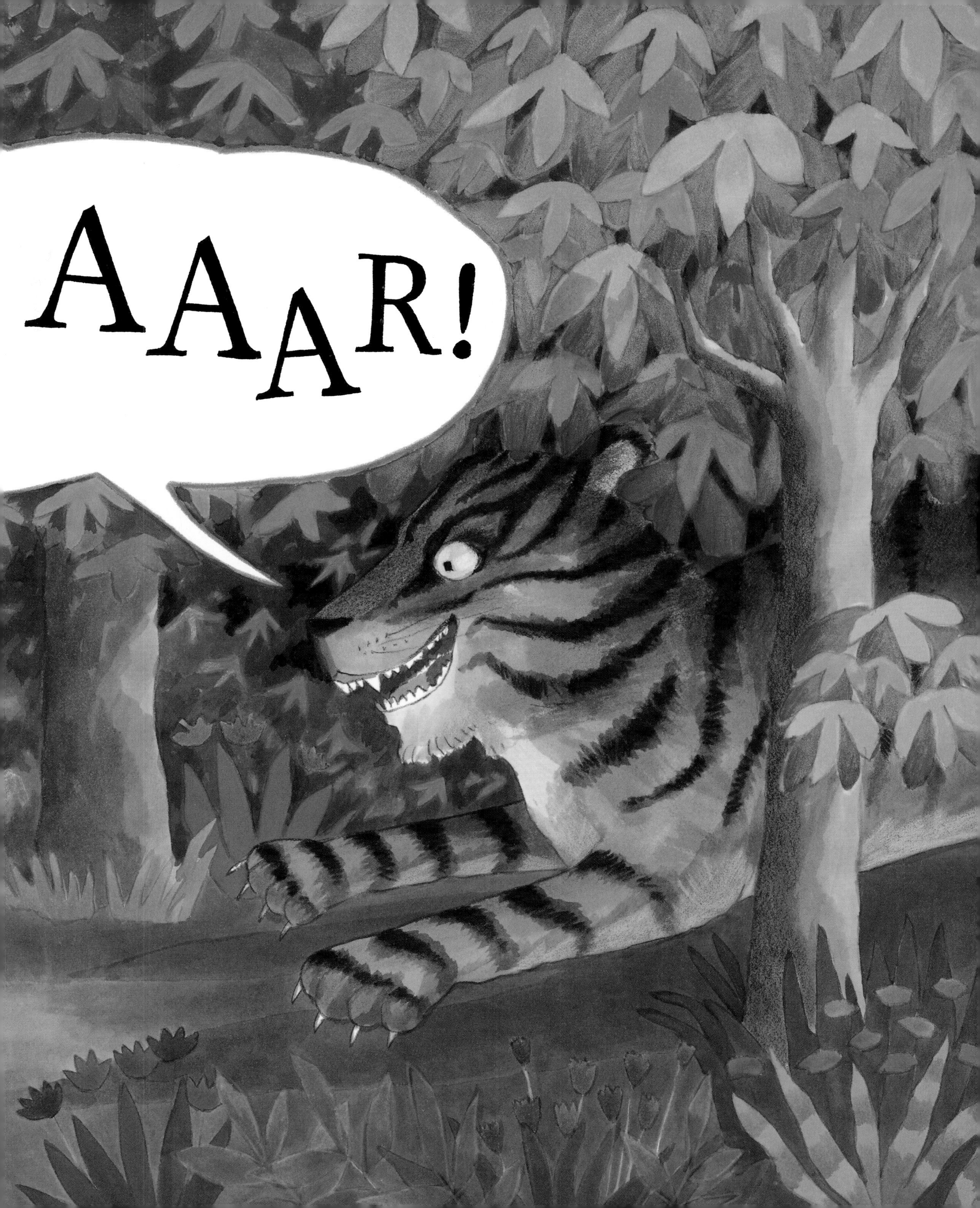
AAAR!

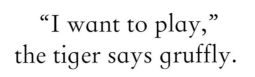

"I want to play,"
the tiger says gruffly.

"Well," says the boy,
"just let me see . . ."

"All right," he says slowly.
"You are the leader,
but the rules of the game are . . .
you MUST NOT turn around!"

The tiger roared,
"READY?"

. . . out of the woods,
shouting and roaring,
follow the leader!

Across the stream,
splishing and splashing,
follow the leader!

Up the steps,
bumping and thumping,
follow the leader!

Round the corner,
jumping and jiving,
follow the leader!

Down the hill,
puffing and panting,
follow the leader!

Over the stile,
leaping and bounding,
follow the leader!

Through the trees,
whirling and twirling,
follow the leader!

Up the path,
hopping and skipping,
follow the leader!

Through the gate,
quickly and quietly,
follow the leader!

Close the door,
grinning and gasping,
follow the leader!

See him go,
dancing and prancing,
follow the leader!
Follow the leader!
Follow the leader!
RRROOOAAr!